KAIJU APOCALYPSE

ERIC S BROWN
JASON CORDOVA

KAIJU APOCALYPSE

The Red Shiva battalion had been composed of five hundred troopers when it marched out of Pacifica Base, each member of its ranks wearing their state of the art "Dogkiller" armor. Accompanied by two fellow battalions, the Death Walkers and Stirling's Peace Makers, they moved into position along the coastline. The base's sensors had detected a vast movement of Kaiju beneath the waves and Red Shiva was there to stop it, one way or the other. They hunkered down and waited for the inevitable attack. Seconds turned to minutes, which turned into hours. Nerves began to fray as the day turned to night. Voices began to mutter in complaint over the comms, openly questioning whether the sensor readings were wrong again. Their guard began to relax as the men and women of Red Shiva began to wonder if it were only a drill. Rations were handed out and eaten, and shift breaks began.

It was then that the Kaiju struck.

The force that rose from the depths was almost unimaginable in size, larger than anything that any living man, woman or child had ever seen. Kaiju poured onto the beach in vast numbers, a veritable flood of claws and fangs, of fury and blood. The fifteen hundred men and women were all that stood against the tide of death, and it simply was not enough. The Kaiju slammed into them with primal fury. Within moments, half of the Red Shiva battalion was simply gone.

"Lay down suppressive fire on the left flank!" Commander Hall was shouting over the comlink inside Jorg's helmet. Jorg turned to see dozens of the Kaiju charging in that direction. The AI of his suit was already acquiring target locks on them as his armored hands brought the massive Mag Cannon he carried to bear. The gun was a product of the Kaiju war. Even the smaller Kaiju were nigh unstoppable. The Mag Cannon fired rounds several times more powerful than those of an old world .50 caliber. It was both a fully automatic weapon, fed from a belt that stretched outward from the back of the Dogkiller suit into its side, and a single shot one. The single shot rounds were carried within a magazine that attached under the forward length of the gun and they were even more deadly. The uranium-depleted shell in each round was filled with a tungsten core, which completed the kinetic round and made it far more effective than the ancient .50 caliber rounds. The Mag Cannon's internal magazine only held five shots of the larger 105 caliber rounds, usually kept in reserve for larger targets, so Jorg opted to go full auto at the approaching Kaiju.

Someone had once compared the smaller breed of Kaiju that were storming the beach to trained dogs and the name had stuck. The Dogs stood between eight and nine feet tall, a mixture of water logged fur and glistening scales covering their malformed bodies from head to toe. They were roughly man-shaped in the fact that they had two arms and walked on two legs, but any resemblance to humanity ended there. The fronts of their faces extended like a dog's, ending a sharpened point of hardened cartilage and bone. Clusters of yellow eyes, much like those of a spider, burned with fury as their demon howls rang out even above the continuous sound of gunfire. The scales mixed with and beneath their hair served as armor. Some had hands that ended in overly extended fingers tipped with razor sharp talons while others possessed no hands at all. Instead, one or both of their arms ended in a giant pincer that reminded Jorg of the crabs he had helped his father catch as a child before the Kaiju arose from the oceanic depths to lay waste to the world, and mankind with it. The creatures swarmed over the Earth like locusts, devouring everything in their path.

Jorg's Mag Cannon spat a stream of death into the Kaiju charging the left flank. The rounds tore through the lightly armored Dogs, splattering the sand with the bright orange blood of the beasts. Wisps of smoke formed where the blood landed, melting the sand, creating a glassy look upon the beach. The Dogs did not notice nor care about their fallen brethren, their stride not breaking as they overran the Death Walkers. Jorg could already see that this battle was lost. The Kaiju were too many and the surface defenders too few. It would be up to the heavier weaponry, which Pacifica Base had, to stop this flood.

The sky flashed yellow and red as the main artillery batteries of Pacifica Base itself entered the fray, precisely on cue. Beams of pure, crackling energy slashed into the main body of the Kaiju forces where the sand met the waters of the ocean beyond. Jorg watched through his filtered visor as the beams swept across the beachhead, leaving deep gouges in the water. The visor was the only thing that kept his vision from being permanently damaged from the energy weapons. Thousands upon thousands of Kaiju died, yet they still came, unceasing. Even the great batteries of Pacifica Base were not enough to matter or change the course of the engagement.

Pacifica Base was one of the last strongholds of mankind, arguably the strongest and greatest. Only Lemura would remain as a true capital of power for the human race when it fell. Lemura, that old rusted bucket, claimed to be the capitol of mankind. Jorg didn't want to die. He was pretty sure he didn't know anyone who did either, so he fought on in the face of hopelessness. "Tango squad, Tango Six. Form up on me and fall back! Repeat, fall back!

Over!" he shouted over his com.

"Tango Six, Red Shiva Actual," Commander Hall's voice came over the comm. "Stand your ground and hold the beach! Acknowledge!"

"Negative, Shiva Actual," Jorg grunted, as he narrowly dodged an attacking Kaiju. He put four rounds into the skull of the offending Dog, and six more in a passing Dog's body. Another Dogkiller, he didn't recognize, punted the beast aside, only to be rewarded by a swarm of the angry Dogs. Jorg opened up on the cluster, killing all of the Kaiju, but failing to save the fallen Dogkiller. "Position is lost. Withdrawing from engagement and preparing for a fortified defense at Location Delta. Acknowledge, over."

Eight Dogkillers came bounding towards him, their thick metal feet leaving deep imprints in the sand behind them. The way he saw it, their only hope of surviving was to get back inside the base. Perhaps there, they could make a stand and keep the Kaiju out of the installation long enough for an extraction group to arrive from Lemura. Staying here on the beach would lead to Pacifica falling before evacuations could be implemented.

A Dogkiller whom his suit's AI identified as Tango 3 took point. Tango 2 and Tango 4 brought up the rear as the squad fought for every inch of ground. The Kaiju were all around them now, a seething mass from which there seemed to be no end.   The battalions had disintegrated in smaller groups of soldiers who no longer tried to hold the coastline but were merely trying to stay alive.

A Kaiju came snarling in from the squad's right as the Dogkillers raced for the base.   Sparks flew from Tango 5's helmet as the Kaiju's talons raked against his head.   The blow must have snapped the neck of the man inside the suit, because Tango 5 spun and fell to the ground. He lay unmoving on the sand as Jorg put a burst of fire into the attacking Kaiju's skull.   The thing's head exploded like an overripe melon, chunks of bone and orange blood spraying into the air.   He quickly sprayed gunfire in the area behind the group, felling a large cluster of Dogs.

The Kaiju behind Tango Squad were gaining ground quickly.   Tango 2 and Tango 4 turned to engage the beasts, their Mag Cannon hosing the front line of the horde of creatures.   Dozens of the Kaiju fell, their guts and entrails leaking from their shattered, mangled bodies, but those behind them pressed onward.   The Kaiju were mindless things, driven by hunger for human flesh and a feral madness so deeply within them, it was a part of their bones.   One moment, Tango 2 and Tango 4 were holding their ground, the next they had vanished beneath a writhing swarm of Kaiju that washed over them, sweeping them from their feet. Jorg shut off his com so he didn't have to listen to the screams of the dying men as pincers and claws pierced their armor, tearing them limb from limb.

Tango 7 and 8 were gone too, lost in the chaos. Jorg had no idea what had happened to them. His attention had been focused on the deaths of his other two squad members to even record their manner of death. Tango 3 was still up ahead of them though, picking his way through the Dogs so that they could make it to the fortified defensive position known as Delta. The servomotors of Jorg's suit whined as he poured more power into them, trying to catch up to Tango 3. They were close to the base. Just a little further and they would be protected by the massive walls of the base, safely ensconced at position Delta. Once inside, they would be able to hold out longer, hopefully long enough for Lemura to send a large enough rescue to pull them out.

A roar louder than thunder shook the night as the ocean beyond the beach began to froth and steam. Out of the waters, a "Mother" Kaiju appeared and began to wash slowly onto the shore. She stood at least two hundred and fifty feet tall. The tentacles emerging from her back that ran down the length of her spine on both sides of the jagged plates of bone protruding outward there, slashed wildly about in the sky above Jorg. She let out an earth-shattering roar, each fang protruding from her mouth larger than a Dogkiller suit. On each hand were four long, spindly claws, obviously designed for rending and tearing. He watched in stunned horror as she moved towards Pacifica Base, her heavy weight shaking the ground beneath his feet, large waves crashing onto the shore as she took step after debilitating step. The base's main batteries swiveled, coming to bear on her. Beams of energy crackled through the air once more as the artillery fired. They blew hunks of flesh from the Mother's chest, causing her to pause and emit a shriek of pain so loud, it blew out the protective sound dampening unit of Jorg's suit. He cursed as his ears popped. He felt blood as it oozed out of them, dripping down onto the skin of his neck. A wave of nausea washed over him, and he realized that his inner eardrums had been ruptured by the Mother's cry.

The Mother Kaiju reared up to her full height and charged at Pacifica Base, her yellow eyes blazing like bonfires in the night sky. Each lunging step increased her speed, and Jorg recognized that even if she were to die before she reached the walls, the sheer mass and momentum of the Mother Kaiju would take her through the walls of Pacifica Base. He saw her crash into the base, tearing through its outer walls with those jagged claws as if they were made of paper. Her huge fists smashed the buildings and towers within, as her tentacles flailed about, doing even more damage to the support structures of the wall. His last hope of refuge was trampled and crushed beneath her massive shape.

"No!" Jorg screamed, horrified. Tango 3 was beside him as the smaller Kaiju reached the two of them where they had stopped to watch the carnage that the Mother had caused. Jorg switched his Mag Cannon to single shot, the giant round reducing the closest of the Kaiju to nothing more than a red mist with its first blast. He never got the chance to fire a second. A Kaiju pincer closed about the throat of his armor, cutting through it with the strength of the creature's grip. His still functioning brain relayed the images his eyes saw as his head bounced along the beach before it finally died and there was only darkness.

Two weeks later. . .

"Pacifica has fallen."

The word of the base's fall shook Governor Pietro Lanstum to his core. He laid the report on top of his desk and rocked back in his chair, rubbing the back of his head. The Minister of War, Andre Yeltsin, saw in the governor's eyes the look of a man who had just seen his own death coming for him. With Pacifica gone, the Kaiju would surely target Lemura next. There was no question of that. Though there were many scattered islands that remained in the wake of the great flood that contained human settlements, Lemura was the last of the United World military installations. The Kaiju were little more than beasts but even an animal knew a threat when one was present.

Lemura Base, in its prime, was once the ruling power of the United World. After the great flood reduced the land masses of the Earth to scattered islands, separated from one another by the oceans, it had been the capital of all mankind. Its population numbered in the hundreds of thousands and its standing army second to none. Governor Lanstum's predecessor had led the war against the Kaiju from its domed walls. In those days, it was easy to delude one's self into believing that mankind, with the advent of beam weapons, advanced infantry armor, and Antellium Quark power, had a chance of surviving the Kaiju plague. Perhaps even of retaking the oceans some day, but with the passing of time those hopes eroded away. Even before the great flood, oceans covered the bulk of the Earth and they belonged to the Kaiju. No one knew what had awakened the beasts from their slumber. The first Kaiju, a three hundred foot tall mother creature, had wandered onto the beaches of the United States of America and wiped out entire cities before the powers of that time nuked the monster into oblivion. Within a month, five more such creatures had emerged to make similar attacks, driving mankind farther and farther inland.

It had been bad before, but humanity survived. It was dangerous, but humans were tough creatures, ingenious when it comes to war, and the battle stagnated as Kaiju were unable to penetrate deeper into the landmasses. Governments continued to function, and the war looked to be a ceaseless one, with a five mile buffer zone between the seas and where humanity would be safe.

That all changed with the flood. The weather patterns of the southern Atlantic and northern Pacific oceans respectively and abruptly shifted, caused by something unexplainable that the Kaiju did or the toll of mankind's ill treatment of the Earth, and the storm surges came, washing away the land. Rain was endless for months, drowning the crops and changing the landscape as mudslides eroded the overpopulated coasts around the world. The west coast of the United States disappeared, the oceans driving all the way inland until it stopped against the western face of the Rocky Mountains, linking up with Lake Mead and the Colorado River. England completely disappeared, swallowed by the Atlantic and the Thames, save for scattered hills in Scotland. France, Space, Malaysia, China... billions died when the seas rose, and the Kaiju continued their assaults with renewed vigor. Latin American had disappeared, and the Amazon River had devoured much of Brazil. India and Pakistan had both blamed one another for the Kaiju, and nuclear missiles had flown at both the Kaiju and between the neighboring enemies. Tibet, once a forbidden land, had become an enclave of hope and refuge – until the day when two Mother Kaiju had waded ashore and stampeded through the beleaguered land.

Over half of the human race perished in those dark days, but those who survived fought on. The United States became the United World as humanity forgot its petty disputes in the face of extinction. The best and brightest were gathered across the globe on the largest of the remaining islands. There the great bases like Pacifica, Alantaica, Lemura, Iceitca, and Nor-wic were built. Technological growth exploded as humanity's numbers dwindled. Beam cannons replaced nukes as the first line of defense against the mother Kaiju and for a while, they worked, keeping the great domed bases safe.   Human breathed a sigh of relief.

Then the tide of the war turned once more. The smaller Kaiju, the Dogs, began to show themselves.   They were the foot soldiers and cannon fodder of the Mother beasts, and their numbers knew no bounds.   Armies of the Dog Kaiju stormed the great domed cities in crashing waves that began to wear them down in a war of sheer attrition.   Alantica was the first to fall, and in the months thereafter, the others fell like dominoes. Even the state-of-the-art Dogkiller suits weren't enough to stem the tide, and now all humanity had left was Lemura Base. Dilapidated, ancient, rusted and almost ready to fall down, but it was the last hope on Earth.

"We have to do something, sir," Yeltsin said, when he could stand Lanstum's silence no longer.

Lanstum leaned forward in his chair towards Yeltsin.   "What can we do?" he asked, his voice barely above a whisper. Pacifica Base had been the strongest, the most fortified, with three full battalions of Dogkiller suits at its disposal and twice as many energy weapons as Lemura. If Pacifica fell, then Lemura had little chance against the incoming storm.

"I'm not just going to sit here and wait to die," Yeltsin countered.   "Maybe it's time we went on the offensive for a change."

Lanstum's laugh was long and loud. Yeltsin suffered through it out of respect for the man's office. He hid his dislike of the governor well, though he would never deny that the man was good at his job.

"You would have me send what remaining forces we have at our disposal away from Lemura and leave us defenseless when we both know it's only a matter of time until the Kaiju hordes show up on our shores?"

Yeltsin shook his head, keeping his infamous temper in check. "No, Governor, I would not."

"Good," Lanstum snorted. "Because you know what my answer would have to be. What my answer would always be."

"I'm not asking for *all* of Lemura's defenses, sir, only the men and women I need to carry out an assault on the Kaiju Overmind," Yeltsin grinned.

Lanstum blinked. Yeltsin felt the governor's eyes looking him over as if to see whether or not he'd gone insane.

"The Overmind is a myth. Just a wild theory some egghead thought up in a lab somewhere. There is no proof that such a controlling intelligence over the Kaiju exists. If there were some magic bullet to stop the Kaiju, I'd expend all our resources to finding it. It. Is. A. Myth."

"I believe it's real," Yeltsin admitted after a moment. "Do you know of Doctor Bach's research into the Overmind theory? Or the evidence which supports his theory and the conclusion he has drawn up that goes with just about everything we know about the Kaiju?"

Lanstum shrugged. "There is little here in Lemura that I don't know of, Minister Yeltsin. But..."

"No buts, sir. Doctor Bach has managed to conclusively detect a psychic form of energy that appears amongst the ranks of the Dog Kaiju during each of their attacks. Bach believes he has found the means to trace that energy to its source."

"And I take it you imagine destroying that source will bring the Kaiju armies to a halt and end their relentless attack," the words were more of statement than a question as Lanstum spoke them.

Yeltsin nodded. "Cut off a snake's head..."

"I see your point, Yeltsin, I do. You've been in search of a miracle to end this war, and you think you've found it in Doctor Bach's work," Lanstum said carefully, "I, however, am a realist, and it's ultimately my responsibility to keep the people of Lemura safe. More so now than ever, as we are the last. If Lemura falls, the scattered, small colonies of man will surely crumble in our wake."

"I understand that, but if I am right..." Yeltsin pleaded.

"If you're right, then perhaps you *could* end this war with a single, decisive blow to the Kaiju."

"Fine," Lanstum relented. "Tell me your plan, and what you need, and I'll consider your request."

****

Technical Specialist First Class Ryan West sat staring at the lump of white and gray that was supposed to be potatoes on his plate. It rested next to the green soupy stuff that the cooks claimed to be the main course of his meal. He picked up his fork and poked at it, uncertain.

"Hey! West! You gonna eat that or what?" Sergeant Parris' voice boomed from across the table. Parris was a big man, and everything he did ended up being loud. Talking, eating, killing. A good man in a fight, though, West allowed. Parris was so big that his Dogkiller armor had to be specifically remodeled to accommodate the well honed mass of muscle that he was. Parris glared at West, waiting for an answer.

Food of any kind that wasn't fish or some sort of kelp was hard to come by these days, and West still couldn't eat fish. The smell of it reminded him too much of the stink of Kaiju. The things stunk so bad up close, not even the atmosphere scrubbers of a suit of Dogkiller armor could keep one safe from the odor. It wasn't the smell of Kaiju, or the potato substitute, or even the green soupy stuff that had ruined his appetite. He had pre-mission jitters, and he knew it. If he ate the pseudo-potatoes, he'd just spray them all over the inside of his armor when he geared up. With little hesitation, he scooted the plate towards Parris. "Have it," West told the big man.

Parris took the plate greedily and started shoveling the white stuff into his gaping maw.

"You spooked or something, kid?" Parris asked as he chewed with his mouth open. Bits of the potato substitute flew from his lips as his words came out.

"Aren't you?" West asked. "It's no secret that Pacifica fell two weeks ago. The news is all over the World Net."

"Lemura ain't Pacifica," Parris growled. "No Kaiju have *ever* gotten through these walls and they ain't gonna."

"Doesn't really matter to us, does it?" West frowned. "We're heading out and leaving the city behind. No walls for us."

"Where did ya hear that, kid?" Parris was clearly surprised by what he'd said.

"I have a friend in logistics," West smiled. "Based on the manifest of equipment, they're getting ready for us, there ain't no way this is just a patrol or special defense duty."

"You have a *friend* in logistics, eh?" Parris grinned at his own cleverness. "Would that be the cute redhead I been seeing you hanging around with?"

West felt his cheeks flush. He ignored Parris' question and cleared his throat before continuing. "Maybe they're assembling an extraction unit to save those they can from Pacifica. I mean, they had some top-notch Dogkillers over there. They'd sure help out around here. That's the best I can figure, anyway."

"Don't matter where we're headed. One Kaiju is just as good as the next when it comes to blowing the fraggers away."

"Yeah, sure," West said, seeing that he wasn't going to get any speculation out of Parris. The big man just didn't think about things like he did. For him it was simply kill. "Catch ya later."

West got up from the table and headed towards the barracks. There were still a couple of hours until their squad was slated to ship out, and getting a little extra sleep was never a bad idea.

****

West stood at parade-rest in the bay alongside the rest of his squad. There were three other squads present as well. No one seemed to have a clue where they were shipping out to. They'd been ordered not to suit up and that fact alone was driving West to distraction. It didn't make any sense. Wherever they were headed, Dogkiller armor was called for. *What use is a Dogkiller without his or her armor?*

"Atten-*hut!*" a voice bellowed out. West, along with every other man and woman in the room, snapped to attention. He perked up with attentiveness as Minister Yeltsin entered the bay. *What in Hades?* West thought. The Minister of War, possibly the most powerful man in all of Lemura, had shown up to address a mere platoon? In all his experience, he'd never heard of that happening. Whatever was going on, it *couldn't* be a good thing.

Yeltsin walked down the line of gathered soldiers, inspecting them. His expression was that of a man playing his last hand in a game where the odds were stacked against him. When Yeltsin reached the end of the line of troops, he doubled back to stand facing the center of the line of the four squads.

"Parade rest!" the same voice called out and West relaxed slightly, shifting his right foot out and placing his hands on the small of his back. His eyes locked onto Yeltsin as the Minister began to speak.

"I'm sure you're all wondering what your mission is," Yeltsin's voice echoed off the metal walls around them. "I'll put it to you as simply as I can. In the next hour, you'll be leaving Lemura. Not for Pacifica, as some of you may have speculated about. You'll be boarding a pair of Tridents. . ."

It was all West could do to keep himself from whistling at that statement. Tridents were the fastest, most combat capable vehicles in use by the United World joint military. Tridents were originally designed as interceptors to engage Mother Kaiju before they made landfall, but ended up becoming the du jour combat vehicle for anything that involved raining death and destruction on Kaiju from the skies. The planes were also submersibles, able to shift from air to water, and could engage the Kaiju below the waves as well as above them. Each individual Trident packed the firepower equivalent to that of a squadron of old world F-16s. The downside of the Tridents were that they cost a fortune to make, and often became the primary focus of a Mother Kaiju in a prolonged engagement. Because of their rising cost, as the war with the Kaiju escalated, the Tridents were phased out of production in favor of more ground based defenses in the city domes themselves. With

Pacifica gone, it was likely that the half dozen stationed in Lemura were the last ones left on Earth. If the brass was planning on deploying two of them, instead of holding them in reserve as a means of escape for the politicians and scientific personal should Lemura fall, it definitely meant something big was in store for them.

"We don't know the exact location of your target at this time," Yeltsin admitted. "But it is a vital one. Perhaps the most vital target of mankind's entire war with the Kaiju, if our calculations are correct. The target? The Kaiju Overmind."

Yeltsin paused as if to allow his words to sink in before he continued. "Doctor Jacoby Bach, the world's leading expert in Overmind theory, will be accompanying. He believes he has found a means to locate this intelligence controlling the Kaiju. Your job, once the doctor completes his, is to make sure that the Overmind is destroyed. By any means necessary, people. By any means."

West was no scientist but he knew enough to understand the Overmind theory. It assumed that there was something out there that humanity hadn't encountered yet. Something that telepathically linked all the Kaiju into a sort of unified hive mind. Doctor Bach and Minister Yeltsin had to be gambling that taking out whatever that controlling force was would at best stop the Kaiju in their tracks or at worst shatter their unity, leaving each

Kaiju a mindless drone with no focus, West reasoned. If they were correct, it would be a decisive victory for mankind. And if such a thing existed, West didn't want to think about the great lengths the Kaiju would go to in order to guard it and keep it safe.

"You will not be issued standard Dogkiller armor for this op," Yeltsin told them. A huge section of wall slid open behind where the Minister stood. West's eyes grew wide as he found himself staring at twenty-four suits of armor which were unlike anything he had ever seen. They were obviously Dogkiller suits, but were sleeker and taller than anything West had worn before. They bristled with armament and were painted a matte black, which seemed to absorb the light in the large room. He couldn't wait to get inside and see what sort of wizardry the computer geeks had come up with to complement the exterior look. "Gentlemen and Ladies," Yeltsin continued, "allow me to introduce you to the Dogkiller Mark II. It has a new, faster, more balanced synaptic interface that doubles each suit's reaction time. The armor of the suits themselves is composed of an experimental alloy called Xantranium which offers a far greater protection against the acidic nature of Kaiju blood as well as producing less exterior heat than anything we've previously managed. The old standard issue Mag Cannons for the Mark Ones have been upgraded as well. The new Mag Cannons, built specifically for the Mark II suits, now contain an internal, revolving 105 caliber chamber. This chamber allows each cannon to carry an additional five rounds. The Mark II's superior strength enhancement and balance alignment augmentation more than compensate for the additional weight of the rounds in combat. The Mark II Dogkiller armor is also the fastest combat suit ever designed. It can sprint for short periods in excess of sixty miles per hours before needing to give its cooling systems a chance to do their job, and can sustain a constant speed of forty miles per hour for as long as your fuel holds out."

West stared at the Mark II suits in awe. They were a grunt's wet dream in terms of firepower and speed, if what Minister Yeltsin said was true.

"Their overall controls are identical to the Mark I suits so adjusting to their use shouldn't be a problem. At any rate, there is no time to run sims in them. It's learn as you go, I'm afraid. I have faith in each of you that you will be able to manage this, or you wouldn't be here. Your squads are the best Lemura has available. I expect success, ladies and gentlemen, for if you fail, Lemura will surely fall with you," Yeltsin finished. "Godspeed, and may He have mercy upon us all."

"Atten-*hut!*"

West snapped to attention, excited, determination coursing through his veins. The men and women in the Dogkiller squads had waited for this moment for a long time. This would be their best shot at truly hurting the Kaiju, to avenge every single loved one and comrade they had lost over the years. It was a defining moment, and West couldn't wait for his chance to bring the pain.

"Fall out and get fitted into your suits! Squad leaders, get your people to docking bay four by 0800!"

As the squads moved to suit up in their armor, West noticed Cathe Smith amongst the members of the other squads. He did a double take as he saw the rank bars of a squad leader on the sleeve of her uniform. It had been some time since the two of them had spoken. After their break-up, West had given her a wide berth, hoping that eventually she'd cool down and they could be friends again, maybe even more. It hadn't happened yet, and he was beginning to doubt that it ever would.

Smith belonged to Alpha Squad, so she wouldn't be aboard the Trident that Gamma and Zeta Squads were assigned to. He supposed that was a good thing. He knew she was professional enough not to let whatever feelings she continued to harbor towards him interfere with the mission but when the squads linked up again wherever they were all headed to, there would be no escaping her.

****

Staff Sergeant Smith suited up, testing out the controls of her new Mark II Dogkiller suit. She clenched and unclenched her left fist as the thick, servo powered armor covering it responded to her neural input. Smith, like every other man and women selected for the upcoming mission, was a longtime veteran of the war against the Kaiju. She was young, a mere twenty two, but the last four years of her life had been spent mostly inside armor and on the front against the Kaiju.

Her body count was staggering, a number that was usually associated with tactical nuclear strikes. She was a lethal machine on the field, moving with an ease and grace that had left many in awe of her skills. Behind her back, some whispered that she wasn't really human, but a last-ditch genetic experiment by the old Federal Republic of Germany to fight against the Kaiju which had risen from the depths of the Baltic Sea before that country, and all others nearby, were systematically wiped from existence. The rumors had also led to her nickname: *Volksrächer*.

West's presence among the twenty-four soldiers deploying had not escaped her notice. Upon seeing Ryan, her guts twisted and went cold. Their relationship had been the rough and tumble sort that combat soldiers often filled the void between ops with. Yet, with West, she admitted to herself, she opened up. The geeky combat tech might be sloppy in the bedroom, but there was something about him, a childlike sense of wonder and a wide-eyed excitement that she had found infectious. As dark and terrible as the world had become with the Kaiju war, somehow West still found a way to see the beauty around him. No matter how much he pretended otherwise, the man was a romantic at heart. She often thought that if she had chased him a bit harder, maybe made a little more effort, their relationship could have grown into something beyond anything she had known before. However, the war, as it always did, messed everything up. West was reassigned to Gamma Squad when a Dog Kaiju shredded that squad's tech. Smith could have requested a transfer and followed him, but she was next in line for command of Alpha Squad. Alpha, being the best of the best, was the squad to be in. Her ego wouldn't let her abandon the need to prove she was the best, too.

Therefore, she had made a choice. Sometimes, though, she found herself wondering if it had been the correct one.

"All right troopers," she ordered her squad, having adjusted as well as she could to the new Mark II systems, "Haul some tail."

Alpha Squad, with Beta right behind them stomped up the ramp into the Trident that was waiting for them. Members of the squads secured themselves in the Trident's bay and got ready for takeoff. The squad would be making this flight inside their new armor. It would give them more time to piddle around with the internal controls and systems of the new suits before things dropped in the pot. If there really were such a thing as an

Overmind controlling the Kaiju, it would surely be heavily defended. There might not be time to suit up once they arrived.

Smith settled in for the flight. Resting her head against the internal brace of her suit, she closed her eyes. They would have plenty of time to worry about the Kaiju they would be going up against when they were actually in the field. Right now, though, there was nothing to do but get better acquainted with her Mark II or sleep. Even through her suit and the Trident's hull, she could hear the ship's massive engines roar to life and the explosive force of its launch as it left Lemura behind.

****

Minister Yeltsin stood on the balcony of command observation tower and watched the two Tridents take flight. They streaked away from Lemura into the night like blazing rockets targeted at a distant enemy. When the two ships were over the horizon, he turned, walking back inside the tower. It was only by the grace of God that Governor Lanstum gave him the green light for the op. Risking four squad's worth of troopers, no matter how good they were, was nothing. It was getting Lanstum to crack open the Mark II Dogkiller project and to allow all twenty-four of the costly prototype suits to leave Lemura that had been the miracle, that and the use of the Tridents.

As he entered the command center proper, it was a sea of chaos. Tech and comm personnel hurried about in their preparations for the battle to come. The long-range oceanic sensor array had picked up movement in the waters to the east. Not just the normal passing of Kaiju raiding parties, but something much more worrisome. The Kaiju appeared to be massing several miles off Lemura's coast. No Mother Kaiju had been detected as yet, but the number of lesser ones grew with each passing hour. His staff's best guess approximated the Dog Kaiju's numbers to be in the thousands already. Only a fool could look at the data at hand and see anything other than an army amassing for an assault. It would take far more than a few thousand Kaiju of the smaller variety to threaten Lemura, however.

Based on the current rate of growth in the Kaiju numbers, it might take several days before they grew to the point of being a true danger. Yeltsin was tempted to seize the initiative. A strike against the Kaiju already off the coast *would* reduce the beasts' number, maybe even drive them away... but it could just as easily prematurely force the Kaiju's hand. If there were Mother Kaiju, dormant or hiding off the coast, such an attack would surely bring them into action. Lemura had withstood attacks before. What was happening now wasn't totally out of the ordinary. With the fall of Pacifica, Yeltsin couldn't afford to take the chances he might have otherwise. He was willing to admit he was on edge. Making the wrong call could bring Lemura to its knees and end the last stronghold that humanity had. Yeltsin flagged down an assistant to fetch him a mug of what passed for coffee these days. Another officer came up to him and handed over a data chip of the standard daily reports on Lemura's overall state of readiness. As soon as the assistant returned with coffee, Yeltsin retired to his office to look them over.

Taking a seat behind his desk, he shoved the data chip into the reader before him. Holographic images appeared before him, displaying everything from totals of functional Mark I Dogkiller suits to detailed information regarding the status of the base's main cannons, all the way down to the current duty roosters. With a sigh, he took a sip of the murky, black liquid in his mug and began to wade through the reports, making adjustments as he felt they were needed.

****

Doctor Bach sat in the pilot's compartment of the lead Trident. Normally his seat would belong to the ship's comm officer, but she had been unceremoniously booted from the aircraft to make room for Bach and all of his equipment needed to run his device. The Trident's bay was filled with the two armored squads of Dogkillers the ship carried, not including the loader, which meant that if the ship had communication problems, they would be out of luck. The men and women in the bay were silent, their thoughts solely on the upcoming mission.

The console in front of Bach looked like someone had gone at it with a sledgehammer and then tried to reassemble while completely intoxicated. Wires dangled here and there from open panels. Entire circuit boards were exposed with additional high tech modulating units jerry-rigged onto them. Despite the mess, Bach felt confident everything was working, as it should. His modifications had turned the standard communications station into a "Kaiju Tracker." Instead of detecting and transmitting radio and laser data, the console now was capable of picking up the subtle, almost surely psychic energy that passed between Kaiju when they communicated with the Overmind controlling and directing them.

Captain James Thornton and his copilot, Lieutenant Commander Marquis Calloway, shared the cramped space with him. Neither of them was overly happy with Bach's modifications to their ship, and was less than enthused with the overall plan.

"Lemura Tower, this is Trident One, over," Calloway said as the lead Trident screamed through the sky.

"Trident One, Lemura Tower has you five by five, over."

"Roger that, Lemura Tower. Commencing stage one flight in one-five seconds, over."

"Affirmative, Trident One. Good hunting. Lemura Tower out."

"Break trans, Trident Two, this is Trident One.

"Go."

"On my mark, begin stage one ascent."

"Roger."

"Five... four... three... two... one... mark!"

"Have you figured out where we're headed yet, Doc?" Thornton asked as he guided the Trident into a steep, rapid climb, with Trident Two mere feet from his wing. The two aircraft flew with a precision that would have been envied by stunt pilots of yesteryear. He added more thrust, as both of the aircraft climbed higher into the atmosphere. Trident Two matched his speed and course, the flight path programmed in before Thornton called off the first mark. The powerful engines howled in response, the g-forces pressing the trio deeply into their seats.

Bach shifted nervously in his chair. So much was riding on this mission that he couldn't afford to be wrong. "Just keep heading east, Captain. There's a very large cluster of Kaiju about an hour out from us. The cluster is too large to be merely a migrating swarm, and the psychic energy readings I'm picking up from that location are off the charts."

Captain Thornton raised an eyebrow. "Ya know, Doc, after all these years on the defensive, I never imagined I'd be hunting Kaiju like this."

"You're both crazy," Calloway spoke up, his eyes never leaving the radar display before him. "This is insane. That's what it is. I mean, if you're right about all this psychic energy junk, we're flying straight into the heart of Kaiju central. I think I'd rather just set a course for Hell and be done with it."

Thornton laughed. "I see your point, but come on, Calloway, we're making history here."

"Yeah, history," Calloway frowned. "How many living historical figures do you hang out with?"

An alarm sounded from Dr. Bach's console. He spun his chair around to take a glance at the readings coming in. His mind quickly disseminated the information. The spiking algorithms were correct, behaving exactly as his computer models had predicted they would. He swallowed nervously as he brought up the overlay and compared the model to the current feed he was reading. They matched. This was it. He knew without a shadow of doubt that he had just located the Kaiju Overmind.

"What's up, Doc?" Thornton asked.

Bach whirled around back to face him with a wide grin as the data he had just uploaded to their stations hit the ship's main screen. "There it is, gentlemen. That tiny island is the location of the Kaiju Overmind. I suggest you take us in and let the troopers in the bay take it from here."

"Wait... you didn't plan for an insertion?" Thornton looked at the scientist incredulously.

"What do you mean?" Dr. Bach asked.

"Sorry, Doc. We can't simply drop in, hit the beach, and unload the Dogkillers," Calloway added. "We wouldn't make it within five hundred feet of that island like this. There's probably a ton of Dogs down there, plus who knows how many Mothers are lurking off the island's coast."

"What?" Dr. Bach said in utter surprise.

"It's not like these Tridents have cloaking devices doctor," Calloway explained. "We head straight for that island and every Kaiju on and around it will swarm us. Only the troopers be toast, but odds are they'd find a means to take us down too, even if we don't actively engage them."

"Oh," Bach slumped in his chair.

"This mission is scrubbed," Thornton said. "Let Trident Two know that the mission is aborted and we need to head back to base."

"Wait!" Dr. Bach snapped his fingers. "What did you say?"

"I said the mission is scrubbed," Thornton repeated.

"No, before that?" Bach turned to Calloway.

"These ships don't have cloaking devices?" He guessed.

"That's it!" Dr. Bach exclaimed. "I'm a fool. Give me an hour before you do anything."

"That's gonna be stretching the limits of our fuel if we want to have enough to make it back to Lemura," Calloway warned.

Thornton checked the fuel gauge and did some quick mental math. "You got your hour, Doc, but that's it. Our return trip is gonna force us to tap into our reserves. While you're doing whatever it is you're doing, we'll follow the SOPs and go over the long range sensor data. It might at least give an idea of what we're up against and how to get the troops where they need to go."

Dr. Bach barely heard Thornton speaking. His

mind was already lost in a sea of possibilities he'd never considered before and his hands flew over the keypad of his console.

An hour later, the two Tridents were circling the island at a respectable distance. Calloway was fiddling with the comm while they waited for Dr. Bach to confirm that his plan was ready.

"I think... I'm ready," Dr. Bach finally said, interrupting the relative silence.

Thornton glanced over at Dr. Bach. "You really think this is going to work?"

"The theory is sound and my models suggest that it will work," the scientist assured him. "There's no reason why it shouldn't."

"So you're telling us you've built a real cloaking device in an hour, with only what you had on hand?" The disbelief Calloway felt was clear in his tone.

"Not exactly," Dr. Bach explained. "I didn't build anything. I just rewired my Kaiju Overmind detector, if you want to call it that, into more of a transmitter. You see, as we approach the island, I'll be blanketing the area with what you would call white noise, like an old electronic jammer. It'll confuse the Kaiju, Lord willing, to the point that they never be able to distinguish us from their swarms. The only risk we run is if the Overmind determines that the blank spot is a danger. It's something to keep in mind."

Thornton shook his head. "You're either a real genius, Doc, or a certifiable madman. I'll let you know when I figure out which. Start up your gizmo and let's get this over with."

"My pleasure, Captain," Dr. Bach grinned and flicked on his hastily rewired again comm. system. After a second, he said, "You're good to go."

Thornton nodded at Calloway, who switched the comm back on.

"Trident Two, Trident One, stand by for Stage Two."

"Roger."

Calloway flicked on the internal comms of the ship. "Dogkillers, listen up. Insertion in five minutes. Be prepared for a splash and dust. Loader at the ready."

The loader, a technical sergeant seated in the cargo hold area with the Dogkillers, swung up from his seat and clipped on his safety tether. He gave it a quick tug, was satisfied that it would hold him, and then he slowly ambled back to the drop door of the Trident.

"Listen up!" the loader ordered as he overrode

the comms of the Dogkillers. "You do not go until I give the signal. Once I give the signal, unass out of my bay and move away from the ship. You do not want to be under the exhaust fans when we depart. If you hesitate, you will die. Do you read?"

"Oorah!" came the shouted reply.

"At the ready!" the loader ordered. The Dogkillers popped to their feet as the Trident began to enter a steep, fast dive. The loader grabbed onto an overhead bar and waited until he felt the ship leveling out.

"Splashdown!" came the call as the two ships hit the water at just over ninety kilometers per hour. The Trident quickly began to sink as the two ships became submersible. The ships shuddered as the engines switched over to pass water through them, momentum slowing briefly. The engines completed their turnover and the two Tridents began to make their way towards the island, less than ten meters beneath the sea's surface. Cavitation from the bubbles shooting out from the wash of the engines began causing the Trident to shake, softly, at first, then harder as they increased speed.

"Breaching!"

The Tridents quickly rose and beached themselves on the rocky shore of the beach. Engines whining as both ships began to turn, the loader dropped the rear bay door open. He held up a hand as he waited, his eyes locked onto the indicator above the open bay. Moments passed before the red light switched to green.

"Go! Go!" the loader shouted. "Get your ass off my ship! Move!"

The Dogkillers quickly disembarked and spread out on the shore, securing the beachhead as Gamma and Zeta squads disembarked from the second Trident. The engines on both Tridents began to howl as the last Dogkiller left the cargo bay. Up in the front of Trident One, Calloway nodded as his loader checked in.

"Dogkillers away! Closing the bay door!"

"They're away," Calloway confirmed, glancing at the sensor data on his screen. The display confirmed that both squads were off the ship and on land. He blinked. "Holy shit. I've got five massive signatures on sonar! Marking them now... Mothers! Repeat, we have Mother Kaiju!"

"Warn Lemura Tower, and let the Dogkillers know as well," Thornton said. He looked at the nervous scientist. "Relax, Doc, we can outrun any Mother."

"Lemura Tower confirms five Mother Kaiju," Calloway said moments later. "Alpha Six acknowledged receiving information as well and is advised. She's passing the information to the other squads. Trident Two confirms our readings and is ready to bug out."

"Good," Thornton said in a hurried voice. "Let's get the hell out of here before the Kaiju realize that we're here as well."

"No arguments from me," Calloway grunted as the ship rocketed out of the water and clawed for air.

****

Alpha Squad took point as the squad hit the beach. Gamma and Zeta squads followed in their wake with Beta bringing up the rear. Dr. Bach informed them of what to expect in a rushed briefing over the comms as the ships orbited the islands before they began the final stage of the insertion. Even so, seeing it was far different from hearing about it. Smith watched the dozens of smaller Kaiju patrolling the shoreline looking through them and passing them by as if the four squads didn't exist. The Kaiju signal the Doc was broadcasting sure had the buggers messed up. She saw one pair of Kaiju turn on themselves. One clawed at the other, trying to gouge out its eyes, as if it were an armored human. They screeched at one another, their confusion evident. She smiled.

Smith called up the location of the squads' target on her view screen. The source of the heightened Kaiju psychic energy that the Doc believed was the location of the Overmind was buried deeply within the island. That made sense on plenty of levels. By being placed in such a fashion, it was protected from airstrikes and the paths to reaching it were greatly limited. They were going to be heading underground through some nasty and narrow passageways to get to their destination. Lastly, humanity had not managed to strike at a core cluster of Kaiju like this since the fall of New Orleans.

Of course, they had to survive the beach and reach those passages first. The amount of time Dr. Bach's transmission could effectively confuse the Kaiju was a complete unknown. They hadn't even been fully convinced it would work. Nevertheless, even if it held, their time was limited. The Tridents picked up the signatures of not one but five Mother Kaiju clustered about the island beneath the waves. If any one of them awoke, the Tridents would be toast, and the Dogkillers wouldn't last much longer. The range of Dr. Bach's device wasn't known either, so Smith had two choices: slow and cautious, or barrel ahead.

Nobody had ever called *Volksrächer* timid.

"Squad Leaders, Alpha Six. Let's pick up the pace!" Smith ordered over her suit's comm. "The range of that device is unknown."

The heavy feet of the Mark II suits threw sand and rocks into the air as they hightailed it for the closest entrance to the system of tunnels that ran below the island's surface. Smith didn't like the tactical situation at all. Though the tunnels were far wider than her suit's sensors made her think they would be, they were still so tightly enclosed that, no more than three troopers could stand side by side within them. Given the Kaiju's numbers, it gave the beasts a huge advantage. All the things had to do was a pick a place to make their stand and they could easily stop the squads from advancing. Smith knew she couldn't allow the Kaiju the time to get organized in such a fashion.

There were two Dog Kaiju blocking the mouth of the internal passage leading farther downward inside the cave. Their yellow eyes looked over her and the other members of Alpha Squad. One snorted and the other shook its head in wild fury. The two Kaiju appeared to be trying to wake up from whatever it was that the Doc had hit them with. She didn't give them chance. Smith jerked up her Mag Cannon, using single shot rounds, and reduced the two creatures to pulp where they stood. Their entrails splashed over the cave wall, slicking it with a bright orange wetness.

"Alpha Four, point. Three and Five, cover," Smith ordered. "Beta squad, secure this location. Gamma and Zeta, with me." Smith received confirmation of her orders and turned to lead the charge as the squads raced downward towards the Kaiju Overmind. She was almost certain that Hell awaited them somewhere below.

****

Alarm klaxons rang out all over the island of Lemura. Citizens raced for their homes and designated shelters as panic filled the streets of the domed city. Minister Yeltsin was cursing up a storm in central command. The group of Kaiju off the coast that had been detected turned out not to be the only one. The Kaiju had Lemura surrounded and swarms of the creatures, each numbering in the thousands strong, were converging upon it. Worse, three Mother Kaiju had shown themselves as the attack began. They rose from the waters, juggernauts of sheer, primal power, and followed the lesser Kaiju towards Lemura's defended shores.

Yeltsin had already dispatched every available Dogkiller to meet the lesser Kaiju. Either they would hold the monsters on the beach or fall back to help defend the city if they failed. The Mother Kaiju was what concerned him now. There were four Tridents remaining on Lemura and Yeltsin scrambled them. The great ships lifted through the top of Lemura's dome. Even in the best of circumstances, four Tridents would have a hard time dealing with one Mother Kaiju. With three, it would be nothing more than a minor delaying action. Lemura's main defense batteries slid from their resting places to target the closest of the three Mother Kaiju. The formation of Tridents broke apart as two ships headed in the direction of each of the other monsters.

"All batteries, this is Minister Yeltsin, fire at will!" Lemura's main cannons thundered, shaking the ground beneath the city, as they spat beams of pure blue energy particles. The lead Mother Kaiju, the primary target that the majority of the base's defenses had locked onto, had the beak of a squid and rows of eyes, three long, that ran down the length of the sides of its face. One of its massive arms ended in a pincer and the other a mass of writhing tentacles. Covering its chest and back was the thick armor plating of something very much like the shell of a turtle. The blasts of the cannons hammered into it there, causing the giant beast to stagger. It sunk partially back into the water before it regained its footing and continued to advance. The plates of its shell were slightly charred, but far from punctured. The cannons whined as they rose on their axis to target the Kaiju's head as it loosed a shriek and began to advance upon Lemura once more.

****

Captain Daniel Walker was the senior pilot of the Trident flight, and while he had been pissed initially at being left behind at Lemura, was now more than ready for a chance at a Mother Kaiju. He brought his Trident, nicknamed "Scather" by her flight crew, up high and in the sun, using the bright light to prevent the Kaiju from seeing the ship. He toggled his heads up display and frowned as he inspected the giant, lumbering beast from a safe distance.

The Mother Kaiju looked like a giant, walking shark. A fin as large as the Trident protruded from its spine. Its arms ended in hand-like, three fingered hands and the scales covering its body glistened in the light of the stars above. Row upon row of teeth filled the giant mouth of the creature, and a long tail extended out behind it. Large black orbs on each side of the mouth rotated independently, the eyes lacking any sort of emotion. Walker recoiled a little at the realization that this Kaiju was different from any other he had seen before.

"Not like it matters," he whispered as he twisted the stick, pulling the Trident into a forty-five degree dive. He pulled the ship onto its back. "Trident Flight, this is Trident Lead. Target acquired. Fox Three! Fox Three"

Twin AIM-199 AMRAAM missiles streaked from the Trident towards the beast, leaving a thin trail of smoke behind each as they flew towards their target. The "Kaiju Killers," as they were affectionately known by the Trident crews, locked on the massive Kaiju, using the latest radar information relayed to the Trident from Lemura Base. Both impacted cleanly on the Mother Kaiju and managed to blow chunks of meat from the monster's massive torso. The Mother Kaiju wailed in pain but trudged onwards. Walker flipped his bird back over and clawed for the sky as the Mother

Kaiju hunched her back. Small, blister-like bubbles formed all along her spine.

"What the...?"

The sky was suddenly filled with tiny projectiles as each blister erupted violently. One projectile narrowly missed Walker's Trident, and he managed to get a brief glimpse of it outside his window as it screamed past.

"Holy shit!" his copilot, Commander Sean Osborne, screamed. He had seen it as well. "Did that thing have wings?"

"Get on the horn with Tower," Walker ordered as he twisted the craft while more projectiles shot past. "Tell them that the Kaiju had adapted. We have anti-aircraft Kaiju."

Walker pulled the Trident into a hard turn, angling back towards the Mother Kaiju he had wounded. His targeting screen was cluttered with smaller icons now, nearly blotting out the Mother. His HUD zoomed in on one of the projectiles and he blinked as he identified what he was looking at. He rubbed his eyes and shook his head as the computer confirmed what he saw.

"That's one big flying lizard," he growled and switched over to the 105 cannons.

"Tower, this is Trident Lead," Osborne said

over the comm. "Kaiju has anti-aircraft personnel in the air. Repeat, the Kaiju have launched some sort of creature into the air. Looks like... I am designating the new targets as Dragons. Repeat, new targets identified as Dragons. We have a count of four-five-zero Dragons, over."

He cut the comms and looked over at Walker, who had an incredulous look on his face. Osborne shrugged.

"Not every day you get to name a Kaiju," he pointed out.

"You're insane," Walker said. He flipped back over to the comm network. "Flight, this is Lead. Guns, guns, guns!"

Walker depressed the firing mechanism of the ship's forward cannons with his thumb. The pintle-mounted tri-barrels swung back and forth, spraying the sky with streams of armor piercing, explosive rounds. The firing mechanism tracked every object in the sky, allowing Osborne to prioritize them as they locked on to their target. The new Kaiju began to fall from the sky as the 105 rounds tore into them. Walker smiled grimly.

"No armor whatsoever," he muttered.

"That's handy," Osborne nodded.

"Target acquired," Walker said. "Fox–"

"Incoming!"

Walker was a combat veteran, one of the few who had survived both New Orleans and Las Vegas. His skills had been honed on the white-hot forge of the battlefield. His list of battles was a mile long. London. New York. Rio de Janeiro, twice. Sydney. He claimed to have the reflexes of a cat, and the eye of a falcon. He also had the record to back up those claims. He was arguably the best pilot still alive. Those skills, combined with two lifetime's worth of good luck, were the only thing keeping him and his copilot alive as the smaller, flying Kaiju began to spit out streams of molten metal at the four Tridents.

Walker jerked his stick all the way back and the Trident responded, the aircraft tilting upwards in the sky and rocketing away. The lithe craft had almost made it away clean, but a stray stream of molten metal tore at the undercarriage of the vessel. Alarm klaxons howled as the targeting system of the Trident went down, completely destroyed by the liquid metal. The rudder of the craft began to shake, dropping Walker's ability to maneuver to almost none. He swore and kicked the floor pedals, disengaged the thrust and waited for gravity to catch back up with them.

"Jesus..." Osborne whispered and pointed at the screen. Walker looked at the screen and blanched.

Trident Three, crewed by Lieutenant Commander Etienne Moynier and his copilot, Lieutenant Larry Southard, had been completely destroyed as dozens of liquid metal projectiles tore through them. Pieces of the flaming wreckage crashed to the ground, creating a mockery of a funeral pyre for both warriors, something that the cynical pilots of the Tridents often joked about. Dark humor was what kept them going, although today, it would not be gallows humor keeping them alive. The Mother Kaiju roared triumphantly and continued her march towards Lemura.

"No chutes," Osborne announced as he turned in his seat and scanned the sky. "Repeat, no chutes! Damn it..."

"Weapon targeting system is down completely," Walker announced as the Trident went through a brief moment of weightlessness before the nose of the aircraft pointed back down towards the earth. As they began to accelerate, he pushed the throttles to full and the engines roared to life. "Landing gear is shot. 105 is down, comms are down. We have engines, but we're low on fuel. Not much else we can do now, really, except..."

"Except... what?"

"You want out? You have plenty of time to eject. Hell, you may even survive."

"And land in the middle of that nastiness?

Nope," Osborne said with a shake of his head. "I've come this far. Besides, this is something I never thought I'd hear you say."

Walker grinned. "Prepare afterburners. We're gonna ram that bitch."

"Hell yeah."

Walker put his hand on the secondary throttle, which sat beneath the primary and was almost never used. The Trident, capable of speed six times faster than sound, never really needed to use the afterburners. He wanted to be certain that he had enough momentum and energy behind what he could only think of as a kinetic strike on the Mother Kaiju. Beside him, Osborne jiggled the circuitry of the weapons for a second before he whooped triumphantly.

"Can't fire the missiles," he announced. "But I sure as hell could arm them!"

Walker's grin turned feral. He pointed the nose of the Trident towards a spot right behind the head of the Mother Kaiju. He looked over at his copilot.

"Ready?"

"As I'll ever be," Osborn allowed. "What a way to go, eh?"

"*Bonzai!*" Walker screamed and pushed the

afterburners to full.

The Trident leapt as the higher-octane fuel was pushed rapidly through the pistons of the engine, increasing the power and air-intake. The engines, already pushing out enough energy to rattle the entire craft, doubled the maximum speed of the Trident in exchange for the loss of structural integrity. The craft turned into nothing more than the afterimage of a blur as it struck the Kaiju perfectly, the Trident nothing more than a very large explosive bullet as it burrowed completely through the spine of the Mother Kaiju. Munitions aboard the craft exploded, severing the head from the rest of the massive beast's body, and secondary explosions rent the upper body into shreds.

The massive fireball which erupted from the disintegrated Trident swept through the air, clearing the sky from the Kaiju Dragons as well as charring a few unfortunate Dog Kaiju on the ground. The massive Mother staggered under the blow, not quite realizing that she was already dead as she tried to continue forward. Nerves, finally catching up with her body, caused her to lose a step, then two. She began to fall.

The Mother Kaiju's corpse tumbled onto the sands of the beach, crushing hundreds of Dogs beneath her as she collapsed heavily to the ground. A cheer erupted from the walls of Lemura upon the sight of the massive Mother falling dead. However, they quickly faded as the two remaining Mothers renewed their attack. The artillery crashed through the sky, and the fight raged on.

****

Captain (j.g.) Charles Knight liked to play things safe. Unlike the other Trident pilots, he was not known to be a hotdog, and didn't possess the typical fighter jock attitude that the others wore openly on their sleeves. He was a deliberate, calculating man, which had helped create the image of a man who was in complete control of his faculties at all times.

Now, though, his icy persona was being tested in battle for the first time. Sticking close to his wingman, he brought the Trident behind and to the right of the other aircraft. Ensuring that his wingman's six was clear of any hostiles, he began to engage the few smaller Dragon Kaiju still in the air. The 105 cannon ripped them to shreds, the fine orange mist drifting downward after the guns had ruined their bodies.

"Captain," his copilot, Chris Cox, warned as he brought up the targeting display. He and his pilot, unlike the other crews, had never managed to become close. As a result, the captain's call sign, "Tsumetaikaze", was almost never uttered. It would have been unprofessional, Knight had claimed. Cox wondered if the man was simply too egotistical and vain to allow himself to be called anything other than his rank.

Knight looked over at the display and frowned. The other Trident was lining up to attack one of the strangest Kaiju he had ever seen. The thing had no legs to speak of, the lower body more like an eel's than anything else. Its back was smooth, as were the scales covering the slender length of the beast. Tall spines ran down the length of the Mother's back. Energy crackled over them like lightning dancing in a summer sky. This Mother Kaiju had no eyes. Instead, it had three gaping mouths adorning the top of its head. A tree-sized antenna, like moving hair, wriggled above each of those orifices.

"That's one ugly bitch, captain," Cox said.

"Language, lieutenant," Knight chastised him.

"Trident Four, Fox Three!" came the call over the comm. The lead Trident opened up with a full volley of missiles. Four Kaiju Killers from each ship sped through the air towards the monster. The three antennae-like things above the mouths of the Kaiju began to wave frantically in the air. Suddenly, the lightning which ran down the spines of the Kaiju coalesced into a bright light near the three mouths. The missiles were met by a funnel of energy from the thing's central mouth, a bright blue-white beam of energy which intercepted them. One by one, the missiles disappeared in flames as they detonated from the energy coursing over them.

"Holy shit!" Cox screamed, forgetting his captain's orders regarding foul language.

"I saw what it did," Knight snapped. His hands flew over the Trident's controls as his ship jerked hard to the right, barely managing to avoid the Mother Kaiju's second blast. All three of the thing's mouths hosed the night sky, their fury directed toward the two Tridents still in the air. Trident Four was not as fast as Knight was, and with a flash, the lives of Lieutenants Karl Stodden and Gary Roulston ended. The lead Trident seemed to melt from the heat of the blast. Globs of Trident Four's molten body rained down over the battle, which was taking place between the Dogkillers and lesser Kaiju on the beach below.

Knight felt a familiar numbness drift over him, one he had not felt since his frantic escape during the Battle of Sacramento. The bitter, acrid taste of fear filled his mouth. He felt a growing wetness in his flight pants and realized that he had pissed himself. Tears welled up in his eyes as the weight of the numbness became heavier. His heart began hammering in his chest and his stomach tightened as adrenaline coursed through him. He pulled the Trident into a sharp turn and he began to head back over Lemura Base.

"What do we do, sir?" Cox was yelling at him. Knight knew the man well, despite the barrier he had erected between him and his copilot. There was no hope of him seeing the obvious answer to his question. He was too blinded by his ideology and recklessness. Knight, on the other hand, had already seen how this battle would be played out. There was no hope for them, for humanity. He had one option, but there was a minor impediment which needed to be removed.

"I'm getting out of here," Knight said. "I want to live. I need to find somewhere safe to hide until this blows over."

"What?" Cox shouted, looking at him. "Are you out of your mind? Get back there and fight! Damn you, we're going back, even if I have to take command of this ship myself!"

Knight yanked his sidearm from the holster on his hip and put a bullet into his copilot's brain. The man's head snapped at an awkward angle as bone fragments from his exploding skull bounced off the wall of the compartment behind where he sat. His corpse slumped forward, leaning into the safety restraints that held him in his chair, never knowing what killed him.

A safe place to hide until this is all over, somewhere safe... Knight thought as he accelerated away from the carnage below. He let the pistol slip from his grasp and it fell to the floor, resting in a pool of rapidly cooling blood.

****

"Sir!" one of Yeltsin's officers shouted at him. "Trident Five – Captain Knight – is disengaging and pulling out! We can't get any response on the comm!"

"Let him go," Yeltsin said, forcing his voice to stay calm even as his fists clenched so tightly that his fingernails drew blood from his palms. He'd suspected that Captain Knight was a coward, but never could have imagined that the man would go so far as to flat out turn tail and run during a battle that was sure to determine the fate of the entire human species. He watched the Trident disappearing over the horizon on the command center's view screen and wished he had the resources to spare to blast the ship into twisted, burning wreckage.

Yeltsin shook off his anger at Knight and refocused himself on the battle as a whole. The Dogkillers were already beaten and fighting an organized retreat from the beach back towards the walls of the base. Lemura's main cannons were hammering the Mother Kaiju, but the assault on the two remaining Mothers barely managed to slow them down. They had stopped their charge, slowing them, but the things just kept coming. The techs were telling him that the cannons were in danger of overheating from their prolonged use against the Mothers, specifically the turtle-like Mother, but they were the only things holding it at bay. The second they stopped shooting, there would be nothing left to keep the monsters from slamming into the walls of the base.

There had been no word from Captain Thornton or Doctor Bach as to the status of their mission. Yeltsin knew their ability to locate and destroy the Kaiju Overmind was the only thing that could save them all now. Lemura's defenses were crumbling and within the hour, the Kaiju *would* break through to enter the city.

"Sir!" a voice called out. "One of the primary capacitors for batteries just burnt out!"

"We can still fire though, correct?" Yeltsin asked.

"Yes sir!"

"Then we hold, damn it," Yeltsin growled. "We hold for as long as possible, to our last breath, our dying whisper. I don't care how we do it, but *we shall hold!*"

****

Deep in the bowels of the earth, Specialist West and the rest of the men and women in Gamma squad closely followed the lead of Alpha squad. They moved quickly down the tunnels, pausing only briefly to orientate themselves before they advanced again. Behind them, West could hear heavy gunfire as Beta squad struggled to hold the entrance to the tunnels, their terse and clipped commands in direct contrast to the carnage they were obviously creating nearer the surface.

"Hold," Staff Sergeant Smith ordered suddenly, and West and Gamma squad pressed themselves against the tunnel walls. Behind them, Zeta pivoted and covered the rear.

Intently, West watched the glowing dot which represented Alpha Four, who was further ahead of the main body of Dogkillers. The dot suddenly went from green to red, and then disappeared from view. His auditory sensors had picked up no noise at all, despite the typical echo which seemed to fill the tunnels. While West was still new to the Mark II suit, he could tell when trouble was afoot.

Evidently, so could Smith. "Weapons hot! We got incoming!"

West swallowed. There were no heat signatures which indicated that Dog Kaiju were inbound, but he trusted Alpha squad's expertise. He turned his head and watched Zeta begin to make their way slowly back up the tunnel. There had been a break earlier, and West knew – as every Dogkiller did – that the junction could serve as both a choke point and a potential funnel for Kaiju.

"Gamma Six, this is Gamma Three," West said as he keyed his comm.

"What's up, West?"

"I'm not reading anything on my scanners," he stated. "No heat signatures, nothing. I thought we'd get something down here. I mean, yeah, it's a bit warmer down here, but *nothing*?"

"Wait one," the squad leader said. A minute passed, then two, before his squad leader got back to him. "I won't relay what was said word-for-word, West, but let's just say, you should focus on your job at this time and let Alpha do their job, okay?"

"Uh, yes, Sergeant," West sighed. He hadn't thought that Smith's anger towards him would interfere with her professionalism, but sometimes, you just never knew.

"We got Dogs!" a voice cried over the comm. He recognized the voice from Zeta squad, and he quickly looked at his tactical display. Zeta was being attacked from both sides by Kaiju, which surprised him. The only way the Kaiju should have been able to flank Zeta was by going through the two other squads, and West was fairly certain he would have noticed Dogs running past.

"Impossible," he heard someone else from the squad mutter. West found himself nodding in agreement. There simply was no way that they could have managed such a feat.

"They tunneled through the walls!" Smith announced over all comms. "Gamma, get back there and assist Zeta. Alpha, hold position."

West, along with the rest of Gamma squad, hurried back towards Zeta, whose life signs were rapidly dropping one-by-one. The heavy suits were shaking the tunnel walls with their footfalls, causing a small bit of rubble to fall from the ceiling as well. A larger chunk dropped down onto Gamma Four's suit, which only West saw. He glanced up and saw a small hole opening up in the top of the tunnel. Yellow eyes appeared from deep within the darkness. He stopped running and tried to jump aside. He made it, but only just. The second ambush narrowly missed him, leaving him alive.

Nobody else in Gamma squad survived, however.

A new breed of Kaiju, one spawned from the hellish depths of mankind's worst nightmares, spilled out from the hole in the ceiling. A horrific cross between spiders and slugs poured forth, their yellow eyes burning in rage as they swarmed over Gamma squad. The men and women struggled to fight them off as best they could, but the new Kaiju left acidic sludge everywhere they touched, dissolving rock, armor and human flesh alike. The brave cries of defiance turned to horrific screams of pain and terror.

West began firing at the new Kaiju, his 105 making short work of the ones he could hit. The others, though, were too close to the rest of his squad, and the slime which dripped from the bodies of the Kaiju was rapidly devouring the new armor which the Minister had previously said was nearly impenetrable. He tossed two grenades up into the hole in the roof, and shot the Kaiju that was trying to crawl out. Orange slime and blood fell to the floor, landing with a sickening splat!

The grenades exploded above, the muffled concussions shaking the ceiling and causing part of the tunnel to collapse. He checked his readings but saw nobody else from Gamma still alive. On the plus side, all of the Kaiju were dead as well. West turned and ran back to Alpha squad, his breath coming in panicked gasps.

"Cathe! Cathe! Spider-slug Kaiju! They slime everything and it burns through everything!"

"What are you talking about, West?" Smith demanded over the comm.

"Gamma's gone. Zeta is probably gone, too," West explained as he slowed his approach to the lead squad. He looked back over his shoulder. "Nothing followed. I don't think they realized I escaped, but they were fucking slugs with legs, Cathe. Slugs!"

Smith was silent for a minute before she responded. "Beta is being overrun by Dogs. Neither Gamma or Zeta are responding."

"We gotta be close," West stated as he rounded the final bend in the tunnel. Alpha squad was waiting there for him, guns pointed in his direction–though not right at him, he noticed. "A new breed of Kaiju? This far down? The Overmind has to be close."

"We can't stay here," one of the members of Alpha Squad urged Smith. "Fish or cut bait, Sergeant."

Smith nodded. "Wheeler is right. We need to keep moving."

"Should we move to assist Beta, Sergeant?" Another Alpha member asked.

"Forget that!" West blurted out, interrupting the conversation. "Our mission is the Overmind. If we're not already all that's left, we soon will be."

Smith readied her Mark II suit's cannon, a fresh magazine locking into place. She had come to a decision. "We press forward. I'll take point. West, stay near the middle of the group. Wheeler, take the rear. Let's move!" She shouted, leading the way around the bend in the tunnel.

Smith came face to face with a small pack of Dog Kaiju that had been creeping its way towards the Alpha Squad. Their mouths opened as she slid to a stop and let the automated targeting system that was within the suit track all six of the Kaiju. She let them have it with her cannon on full auto. The rounds tore the monsters apart, spraying the rock walls with their entrails. As the creatures' bright orange blood smoked on the rock, eating away at it, she kept moving. West, ignoring her order to stay back with the rest of the squad, was right on her heels. The rest of Alpha charged after them.

More Kaiju came as they moved deeper, and more Kaiju died. Smith moved like the Grim Reaper, harvesting the dead Kaiju with each step. She was operating in an alpha state now, no longer directly conscious of her actions, merely a passenger as her training took hold. She was the *Volksrächer*, born of a land which no longer existed and a people whose ghosts cried out, and she was going to avenge the billions who had fallen at the hands of the invading Kaiju.

One way or the other.

*****

"Lemura Tower, this is Trident One," Calloway called over the comm as the two Tridents streaked back to Lemura as fast as they could. Static greeted him. He toggled his comm and tried again, with the same results. He flipped frequencies. "Two, this is One. You getting anything from Lemura?"

"Negative, One," came the response. "We've tried all the frequencies as well. Something's jamming the signal."

"Acknowledge, Two. One out," Calloway looked over at Dr. Bach, who was leaning back in his seat with his eyes closed. "Doc. Hey, Doc!"

"Huh? Whuzzat?" the theoretical physicist blinked and yawned noisily. He stretched his legs out and smiled dreamily. "Are we back at the base yet?"

"No," Calloway said. "I haven't been able to raise the base. We're getting some sort of static interference. I think the Kaiju are jamming our signal."

"No, that's just the result of the solar flare hitting the earth." The doctor shifted his body to get as comfortable as he could in the cramped cockpit. "It makes long-range radio frequencies go haywire. Another hour or three and it should be clear."

"What?" Thornton looked over at the physicist now. "What do you mean solar flare?"

Dr. Bach began to explain. "A solar flare is when our sun ejects a corneal mass from the surface, which in turn–"

"Not what I meant!" Thornton interrupted, his voice harsh. "You deliberately chose today to assault the Overmind, knowing we wouldn't have communications once we got out over the ocean and lost our line-of-sight laser comms?"

"Oh, well, yes," Dr. Bach nodded. "My theory suggested that the Overmind works very similar to that of a radio, and I guessed that control of the Dog Kaiju and the Mothers would be weaker today. It's why I had to hurry and get the theory passed. The next solar flare wouldn't have happened for another three weeks by our predictions, and I doubted that Lemura would stand another week at most."

"Jesus..." Calloway muttered. "If you weren't so smart, I'd toss your ass out the window."

Thornton nodded. "Makes sense, I guess, but we had them earlier. Why not now?"

"Curvature of the earth, radiation spikes, the ionosphere playing merry hell with the radio band frequencies, take your pick," Dr. Bach explained. "All these things can and do happen during a flare, especially when a corneal mass ejection occurs. Did you know that, one nearly hit the planet full on in July of 2012? It was a near miss. It would have been worse than the Carrington Event was. Imagine fighting against the Kaiju while trying to recover from something like that. Talk about blind luck, though luck is comparative when looking at it in hindsight..."

"Hey, what's that?" Calloway asked as an unidentified blip appeared on their radar. He toggled the IFF and it blinked blue after a moment of indecision. Seconds later, detailed information flowed across his screen. "Well, at least the radar still works. That's Trident Five."

"Knight? What the hell is he doing out this way?" Thornton wondered as he checked his fuel gauge. They had just enough to make it to Lemura at their current speed. He did some quick mental math before making a quick decision. "Trident Two, slow to eight-five-zero knots, acknowledge." Thornton slowed the Trident down by two hundred knots, which would give them an additional fifteen minutes of flight.

"Roger, One. Slowing to eight-five-zero knots," came the reply from Trident Two.

"We got laser comms with Knight?" Thornton asked his co-pilot.

"Uh... yeah, raising him now."

"Trident Five, this is Trident One. Come in, Trident Five," Thornton said once Calloway had linked their comms.

No response.

"You sure he's receiving?" Thornton asked after a moment.

"He's five-by-five," Calloway confirmed. He double-checked his comms again, and then frowned. "That's weird. Maybe he's suffered some sort of–"

The threat detector suddenly screamed to life, filling the cockpit with a cacophony of noise. Calloway's eyes widened as he immediately scanned the water, looking for any sign of the Kaiju. The ocean appeared to be tranquil below them, however. His eyes tracked back up to the threat radar.

"Holy shit! Two incoming missiles, designating Tango One and Tango Two. Range, one-six miles and closing fast!"

"Who fired at us?" Thornton nearly shouted as he pushed the Trident lower towards the ocean surface. "Was it Kaiju?"

"Knight fired at us!" Calloway yelled as he flipped a switch. "Preparing chaff and flares!"

"Hold one," Thornton said as his heart began to slow down from its frantic pace from moments before. "Neither has a lock on us."

"Trident Two, you have inbound Tangos, do you copy?"

"Both have hard-lock, One," Trident Two replied in a calm voice. At least, as calm as a pilot under fire could be. "Preparing to deploy chaff and flares."

"Knight! What the fuck are you doing? You've targeted allies, you blithering asshat!" Thornton shouted into the comm, ignoring radio protocol in his anger. "Break off your attack, damn you!"

Trident Five remained silent.

"I know you're reading this, Captain Knight. Respond, damn you!"

No response.

"Fine. You want to play games with me, you little shit," Thornton growled. "Sidewinders are armed and seeking, Knight. Don't make me shoot you out of the sky. Acknowledge receipt of this transmission, over!"

"...find a safe place. I just need to find..." a whispered reply broke through the comm.

Thornton and Calloway shared a look. "Are we recording all of this?" Thornton asked, his voice carefully neutral.

"Yep," Calloway nodded.

"Last warning, Captain Knight. Detonate your missiles or you will be fired upon." Thornton leveled off the Trident roughly fifty meters above the surface of the ocean. Trident Two had not followed their descent, choosing instead to try to climb into the upper atmosphere to take the two missiles which had locked onto them. They rapidly moved further from Trident One. He toggled the comm himself. "Trident Five... Knight, listen to me. Destruct your missiles now. You've accidentally targeted Trident Two. You've targeted Commander Tom Coonradt and Lieutenant Robert Head. You know them, they're your friends. Coonie and Gets More? C'mon Knight, kill those missiles."

"Ten seconds," Calloway warned.

"You can't make me go back there," Knight whimpered over the comm. "You can't. You can't."

"Five seconds."

"Deploying chaff and flares," Trident Two announced. "Hitting afterburners... now!"

Thornton and Calloway watched helplessly as the two Sidewinder missiles ignored the chaff and the flares, homing in on Trident Two. A bright flash appeared high in the sky above them, and suddenly, the missiles and Trident Two were gone from the screen. Calloway toggled the comm switch a few times, but was met with static only. The two men sat silently in the cockpit for a minute before they risked speaking again.

"How're we loaded, Cal?" Thornton asked.

"Four AIM-33 Sidewinders," Calloway replied in a cold tone. "We're well within range of him."

"Target his chicken shit ass," Thornton growled.

"Are we... shooting at another human being?" Dr. Bach asked, his voice filled with confusion and worry.

"He's a rutted coward, Doc," Calloway corrected. "Not a human. Sidewinders are targeting... lock! I have a solid lock!"

Thornton depressed the trigger and the two missiles leapt from beneath the stubby wings of the Trident. They rocketed away from the Trident and into the sky, their targeting systems in their data programming locked fully on the other Trident. The three men in the cockpit watched the missiles track through the air as they moved closer to Trident Five.

Knight, for a reason that the three men would never fully understand, did not budge from his level course. His engines ran hot, and his metallic radar signature remained easy to track. No chaff or flares were fired, giving the two missiles an easy time of it. Three pairs of eyes watched the missiles move on their intercept course. Knight continued to run on a straight and narrow path as the missiles accelerated to an intercept, and without much fanfare, Trident Five was blotted out of existence.

*****

The memories of Cathe Smith's long-dead family came to mind as the caverns began to twist oddly around her. Faces appeared and disappeared with maddeningly speed, their visages just at the edge of her mind but never fully brought into focus. It was distracting, but Smith refused to falter. The cold which ran through her veins was born of experience and determination, from willpower and inner strength.

She shook her head. Something was messing with her mind, and she didn't believe that it was any sort of inner doubt. "Alpha, move it!" she kicked a Kaiju in the head, brain matter exploding outwards and showering the rock walls of the tunnel. "We're almost there!"

The tunnel opened into a vast cavern. The sheer darkness of it almost startled her, but Smith had been prepared for the contingency. External lights on her suit kicked on as thermal imagery began to draw a picture of just how immense the cavern was. Teeming around her was thousands of Kaiju snarling, a slathering, howling mass of flesh and anger. Her head continued to swim as she tried to absorb all of the information she saw.

There. She felt, more than saw, the presence which had been trying to overwhelm her for the past ten minutes. Deep in the bowels of the cavern sat something which twisted the walls around it, causing her to feel nauseous and anxious at the same time the longer she stared. Eight arachnid-like legs protruded from its body, supporting the weight of the thing's massive brain-shaped lump of a body. Scores of tentacles, all originating from its central mass, whipped and cracked in the air around the thing. The Overmind Kaiju had no discernible eyes or ears that Smith could see. Its central mass was several times larger than an assault tank. On the upside, she noted, it had no scales or armor of any kind. Other than the thing's tentacles, its body appeared to be exposed brain matter, soft and gelatinous.

"A soft target," she whispered. She opened her mouth to issue commands.

The Kaiju Overmind struck before she could give the order to attack. One of its tentacles shot outward, snagging a member of Alpha Squad who had skidded to a stop to Smith's left. It jerked the man off the ground and proceeded to smash him time and time again into the wall of the cavern, cracking his enhanced Dogkiller armor open like an egg. Blood and fluids from the armor's systems leaked from the damaged suit, but the tentacle continued its grizzly work. A second tentacle shot forward at Smith. She dove from its path, rolling as the metal of her suit clanged against the cavern floor, and brought her cannon to bear. Smith fired a series of three bursts which cut the tentacle to shreds.

West wanted to assist her with the tentacles but the mission came first. He sprinted towards the Overmind, firing with each step he took. The heavy 105 caliber rounds blew gaping holes in the Overmind's central mass, spilling chunks of grey matter and orange blood upon the cavern floor. It shrieked in pain from the wounds, and for a moment, the tentacles waved wildly in the air. The cry was not truly a sound but more of a feeling that forced itself into West's mind, splintering his thoughts. He stumbled and crashed to his knees, the armored hands of his Mark II suit reaching upwards to cover the sides of its helmet. West saw the troopers of Alpha Squad doing the same. The cry was more than just one born of the creature's pain. It was an attack on their minds.

The mind controls all, a small, sane part of West's brain argued as he struggled to regain his senses.

Tears ran over West's cheeks inside his suit, but he fought to overcome the noise tearing his thoughts and will apart. His hand trembling, he managed to raise his cannon in the direction of the Overmind and activate its firing mechanism. He swept the cannon in a side-to-side motion on full auto, hoping to score a lucky hit. The shrieking stopped. West shook his head frantically, trying to pull himself together. Besides Smith, all but one of Alpha squad was down and was not moving. He could feel blood leaking from his eyes, ears, and nose, trickles of warm wetness flowing over his skin.

Even gravity seemed to be doing odd things around the Overmind.

He called out to the rest of the squad. Smith answered, as did Wheeler. Nobody else spoke up. Very likely, the troopers who were down were dead, overwhelmed by the Overmind's psychic attack.

The Overmind reared up. The thing's four hind legs supporting its weight as it scuttled forward to finish them. Smith and the remaining Alpha squad trooper were firing everything they had at the monster on full auto, a single round, and back again. Pieces of the Overmind were everywhere around them. A purplish blood oozed from its central mass and stained the floor and walls of the cavern. The Overmind refused to die though. One of its lifted legs impaled Wheeler straight through the man's chest, passing through his armor with its point emerging from his back. The Overmind shook the trooper's corpse from the point of its leg. It settled back onto all eight legs as Smith's voice broke through the ringing in West's ears. "We have to end this!"

"I'm with you!" West shouted over his suit's comm as he leveled his weapon at the Overmind's central mass and fired the last of his 105 rounds. Again, chunks of the monster exploded and a darker shade of orange blood splashed everywhere. The massive Overmind stayed upright, refusing to fall despite the grievous wounds it had suffered from.

West saw movement out of the corner of his eye. He jerked his head around to see hordes of Dog Kaiju entering the cavern through the entrance he and Alpha Squad had used. There were too many of the monsters to count.

"We have company!" West screamed. He spun to engage the newcomers, a stream of full auto fire from his cannon meeting their forward ranks head on.

"West. . ." He heard Smith say. "I'm sorry. There's no other way."

"What. . ." he started and then realized what she meant as he saw the icon of her suit on his tactical display screen shift from a green dot to one of pulsing red. Smith had set her Mark II to self-destruct. He forgot about the Dog Kaiju and whirled to race towards the Overmind. He saw Smith charging it. She dodged tentacles that slashed out at her and slid like a baseball player between the Overmind's legs. As her armored form skidded to a halt directly beneath the Kaiju Overmind, the world went white. West felt the heat of the blast as his retina were burnt away and the armor of his Mark II melted into nothingness, taking his flesh and bones with it.

He never did get to tell her that he had loved her.

****

The once-grand streets of the city of Lemura had become a veritable warzone. The turtle-shelled Mother Kaiju, whose continued march towards the city proper could not be stopped, had shattered the dome surrounding the city. Yeltsin stared at the monitors in the command post with a mixture of anger, disgust, and fear. For all their effort, the main cannons couldn't stop the monster. The Mother Kaiju was missing an arm, and Yeltsin was convinced the beast was half-blind from multiple hits to the head. The arm on its right side ended in a stump of blackened scales and its face and legs were scorched to the point where the thing's tissues were charred beyond recognition, and yet the beast still stood. There seemed to be no stopping the lumbering Kaiju. The monster limped along, striking at buildings with its one good arm and crushing whatever was unlucky enough to be under its feet.

A division of ancient tanks moved down the primary road to meet the Mother Kaiju as it headed for the heart of the city. In a last-ditch effort, Yeltsin ordered them to target the monster's already wounded legs in the hope of bringing it down. Blasts of flame and smoke erupted from the barrels of the tank's main guns as they thundered in chorus. They struck the Mother Kaiju in its thighs just below the edge of the shell covering the beast's torso. The monster reared back its head in a howl of pain, dropping to one knee. Its remaining arm swiped at the tanks. One tank's side caved inward as the Mother Kaiju's pincer made contact with it. The blow sent the tank rolling into the tank next to it before both exploded in a fiery blast of orange and yellow flames. None of the men and women inside managed to escape before a massive secondary explosion signaled the rupture of the magazine rack within one of the tanks. The second explosion vaporized both vehicles.

Yeltsin was tied into the comm channel the tanks were using. He heard the division's CO screaming for the tanks to withdraw. Both heavy vehicles kicked it into a hard reverse as they fired again. This time, their shots slammed into the hardened armor of the Mother Kaiju's shell with no effect. The Mother Kaiju tried to get to its feet, but failed. Its massive body rocked the street as it collapsed back onto one knee. The two tanks were in the process of turning around for a full out retreat when the giant beast swept its arm through a nearby building breaking apart the top half towards the tanks. The shower of debris hit them before they completed their turn. One tank was covered entirely, the other barely escaping the same fate.

All around the battle with the Mother Kaiju, platoons of infantry engaged the flood of Dog Kaiju that had poured into Lemura through the opening that the massive beast had made for them. The bulk of the infantry troopers wore basic combat gear. Only a few were in Dogkiller armor. Most of the Dogkiller suits available had been lost, along with the men and women wearing them, during the failed attempt to hold the shoreline against the Kaiju swarm. The Dog Kaiju were everywhere. They clogged the streets and alleyways of the city, sweeping through it like a tide of howling death. The chatter of small arms fire mingled with their cries.

One group of either very brave or very stupid soldiers had slung together a barricade made from the wreckage of the city in the main street leading to the city's heart. They fought desperately to hold it against the juggernaut of the Kaiju forces. Yeltsin watched on one of the monitors as the tripod mounted machine guns they'd set up atop the barricade tore the first wave of the Dog Kaiju to shreds. Grenade launchers lobbed explosive rounds into the center of the of the Dog Kaiju lines as the monsters continued to press forward. The soldiers around those using the mounted weapons added the fire of their rifles to the fury of the battle but it didn't matter. The Dog Kaiju were too many and too determined. The monsters reached the barricade and the valiant cries of the soldiers became screams as they were ripped apart by the horde.

The tank that had escaped the Mother Kaiju in its mad flight from the beast had turned onto a street where the Dog Kaiju were swarming en mass. The monsters spotted the heavy vehicle at once and came at it by the dozens. The tank's secondary guns blazed, hosing the creatures with 105 millimeter cannon fire. One Dog Kaiju was cut in half, its intestines spilling onto the street. Another's skull evaporated from a nearly point blank hit. Another paused to stare at the orange blood spurting from its shoulder where an arm had been connected only a moment before. The tank's main gun was useless at such close range as the Dog Kaiju leaped onto its hull, slashing grooves into its armor with their claws. Yeltsin held his breath, hoping for a miracle, as the tank tried in vain to flee. Several of the Dog Kaiju working together yanked its main hatch open. Scale covered hands reached into the vehicle and pulled one of its crew out. The poor woman died painfully. Two of the Dog Kaiju, fighting over who got her flesh, ripped her arms from their sockets as her blood splattered over the green exterior of the tank. A third Dog Kaiju nuzzled its head into her abdomen, its teeth sinking into and tearing the woman's flesh. When she lay still atop the tank and the Dog Kaiju raised its red stained face towards the camera Yeltsin was watching the battle through, the Minister of War turned away.

"Shut that feed off!" he snapped at the closest officer. Nevertheless, Yeltsin knew inside that the grizzly scene he had just witnessed was what lay in store for them all. "There's nothing more we can do from here. What's the status of the east wall?"

"Gone, sir," someone called out. "Dog Kaiju overran the defenders when the auxiliary heavy support units moved out to support the south wall, where the Mother breached."

"North?"

"Holding for now, sir," a new voice called out. "Dog Kaiju are light up there. We've diverted some of the defending units to the east to help, but we're not sure they're going to make much of a stand.

"West is holding as well, sir," an officer reported. "No spare units to redeploy, however. Those flying Kaiju shredded their defenses."

Yeltsin looked back at the various monitors. Command Central had fallen silent around him. All the officers and personnel were staring at him. Yeltsin realized his cheeks were wet with tears. He roughly wiped them away. "I want everyone to grab whatever weapons they can." His voice was harsh, though it did not break. "We're going to be joining the battle out in the streets."

"Sir!" cried an officer who sat at one of the consoles across the room from where Yeltsin stood. "The Kaiju! Something's happening to them!"

Yeltsin turned to look at the monitors that hadn't been shut down yet. The Dog Kaiju had gone insane. Many beasts were attacking each other, tooth and nail, and those that weren't, stumbled and moved awkwardly as if their brains had suddenly short-circuited. All eyes went to the monitor showing the towering Mother Kaiju as the great beast thrashed about wildly. The pincer of its remaining arm snapped open and closed on the flesh of its own face.

Cheers went up all around the command area. Yeltsin felt as if he had just been gut punched. It was one thing to hope for a miracle and a whole other to see it delivered to you. With the Kaiju driven mad by some unseen force, they actually had a prayer now. They could turn the tide of the battle and push the monsters back into the ocean. He struggled to keep his voice professional as he shouted, "To the streets! Long live Lemura!"

With that on the lips of the men and women in Control Central, the battle to reclaim Lemura began.

****

Yeltsin moved through the streets, training from another time and place coming back to him as he led his bastardized platoon through the ruined streets. The Kaiju everywhere were in disarray, but still very dangerous. They quickly found that out as two Dog Kaiju grabbed an unarmored colonel and dragged him off into a darkened alley, his screams loud and piercing until they were abruptly cut off. Yeltsin tossed a few grenades into the alley and moved on.

"This is Lemura Actual," Yeltsin said over an open circuit, tapping his comm into every comm unit in Lemura. "Minister Yeltsin, for anyone confused. I am leading the efforts to take back our streets. If you still have your weapon and ammunition available, I urge you to join me in taking back your city, your home, your life. This is for Lemura. Long live Lemura!"

So rang the battle cry of humanity. Pacifica, Atlantica... they were the fallen beacons, no longer lighting the way for humanity to survive. They were gone, swept away in the oceans of time. They would not be rebuilt. They would be memories of failure, of lost lives, of abandoned hope. They would only exist in song and story, and even then, their importance would be lessened in human history. That was Minster Yeltsin's legacy, and it was one that he was not ashamed to admit striving for.

Gunfire erupted ahead of them. Yeltsin watched as a man and his three sons barreled out of a ruined apartment building, old hunting rifles in their hands as they joined the battle. A lone Dog Kaiju attacked the family, who valiantly fought back. The father was dragged to the ground, ripped apart by the Kaiju. His sons killed the beast. Yeltsin nodded approvingly.

"Now is the time, people of earth," he whispered fiercely. "Now is the time to take back our city, our planet."

A soldier fell, and a citizen took his place. Yeltsin noticed but said nothing to the woman, who was fearfully clutching an old revolver in her hands. There was a steely glint of determination in her eye.

Yeltsin would not discount the woman, or any other person who stood up to fight. This was humanity's final stand, and every man, woman and child capable was a soldier now.

"Forward!" he cried out and led the way, men and women following closely behind him. The Mother Kaiju, severely injured and apparently cut off from the Overmind, was still a severe danger. The small arms would likely do very little actual harm to the massive Kaiju, but even enough bee stings can kill a bear.

The Mother Kaiju roared painfully somewhere nearby as more fire poured into her exposed flank. The turtle shell, which offered near-invulnerability in the front of the beast, did not cover her back as well. The thick scales of the Mother were all that stood between life and death for the beast. He checked his belt for grenades and saw that he had ten left. Others in his growing group had more, and he saw that one civilian who had joined them was carrying a large bundle of claymore explosives. He blinked at that, but refrained from commenting. Survival was important, and how they did it, was not.

"She's hobbled at the corner of Main and Prosperous Street," Yeltsin said over the comm. "Let's bring that big bitch down!"

"Long live Lemura!" came the cry over the comm as thousands of voices responded as one.

The ground around Yeltsin shook. He glanced up and saw that the Mother was still down on one knee, but was struggling slowly back to her feet. He broke into a trot, then a run. They had to keep the Mother from rising, and he wasn't sure he had the firepower to do so. He risked a quick look at his oversized platoon, which was now numbering a few hundred men and women, some in uniform, most not. The frightened woman he had spotted earlier was now carrying the explosive claymores.

He rounded the corner of Main and skidded to a stop. He had managed to make his way to the rear of the Mother Kaiju, where a small group of uniformed soldiers was trying the shoot the Mother in a most indelicate spot. Judging by the way the Kaiju was thrashing about, Yeltsin was sure that the determined solders were starting to make progress.

"Attack!" Yeltsin cried and the men and women around him surged forward. "Do not let what is written on your headstone state that you simply died here! Fight for humanity! Long live Lemura!"

"Long live Lemura!"

A small form, a young girl no more than ten, clutched a small satchel in her arms. She ran forward, darting around the adults as they fought the Mother Kaiju, her bright brown eyes never wavering as she drew closer to the Mother. Her pigtails bobbed as an adult bumped her unknowingly, but her path did not stray. She drew very close to the exposed underside of the massive beast and stopped. She looked up at the Kaiju, and in a voice that belonged to someone ten times her size, made a declaration in a ringing tone:

"Long live Lemura!"

The explosive in the satchel pack detonated, killing the large cluster of humans gathered close to her position. The ball bearings, which had been packed tightly around the explosive material, shot upwards at over fifteen hundred meters per second, the steel penetrating deep into the Mother's stomach. The little girl vanished in the blast, but in the process of dying, managed to wound the Mother grievously.

Men, women, and Dog Kaiju were all turned to mist as the ball bearings made short work of the unarmored humans around them. One bearing blew straight through Minister Yeltsin's pants leg, narrowly missing his thigh. Red blood mixed with orange on the street, and the horrid stink of death and carnage filled the air.

The damage was done, however. The Mother Kaiju bellowed one final time, a cry born of pain and defeat. Her good leg gave out, and the top-heavy beast tottered as her guts began to spill out onto the street. The massive shelled creature began to fall to its side, the heavy creature flattening buildings and killing thousands of people and tens of thousands of Dog Kaiju as she went.

The battlefield became deathly still. Yeltsin stared at the mass in awe at the Kaiju gave one final shuddering gasp before expiring. He felt it in his bones. The blood-chilling roar which had begun from blocks away, one that told him that he had won, that Lemura had won.

The victory cry of humanity was powerful enough to shake the very foundations on which Lemura was built.

Two days later...

Governor Pietro Lanstum was dead, his body somewhere in the rubble of the formerly grand walls of Lemura. Like so many others, the Governor died when the Mother Kaiju had breached Lemura's walls and let the smaller monsters inside. According to the report, Yeltsin had read over, the Governor's personal guard had died to the last man to keep him alive. It simply hadn't been enough, and the Governor had fallen amidst the seething hordes of Dog Kaiju. The whole mess left Minster Yeltsin dealing with more than most men could stand to bear.

He had started smoking again from the stress, luxuriating in the cigarettes he had found hidden deep in the supply stocks of an old storage warehouse. There was vacancy of power in the civil government with Lanstum's death, and no time to fill it properly. The Lieutenant Governor hung herself upon the breach in the walls, though her part of the city had not even been touched, being safely protected by the east wall. After that, Yeltsin had no idea who was still alive.

Over thirty-five percent of Lemura's population had been lost to the attack, and most of its armed forces were dead as well. Entire sections of the city were in utter chaos, ruined beyond repair. In those places, looting, rape, and the law of the gun reigned while Yeltsin struggled to assemble the manpower to restore order. With the high casualty count amongst the military, he was forced to rely on a less-than-adequate police force.

Worst of all, Lemura's primary power grid was completely offline. Teams had worked around the clock to repair it, but the best estimates told him it would be at least a matter of days until any real progress could be seen. In the meantime, the citizens of the city were forced to use oil heat, if one could find it, or risk starting a fire in their homes to keep the survivors fed and warmed. It was not a comforting thought, one Yeltsin knew was at the top of his list of things to accomplish before they could truly say that Lemura still stood, and would remain the bedrock of humanity.

Yeltsin found himself not only Lemura's Minister of War, but acting Governor as well. The collapse of the civil government left him no other choice, and this was one position he did not want to have. He would establish elections as soon as he was able, but since restoring the safety and security of the citizens of Lemura took precedence, he figured elections would occur in three months, at the soonest.

He rubbed his aching eyes. He vaguely remembered what sleep was like as he popped his second stimulant of the day and set aside the report of Lanstum's death.   Lanstum's death was unfortunate, for the man was, if anything, an effective administrator. The loss of his lieutenant was a lesser hit, but still one that he could have done without. There were so many tasks to be completed and no guarantee that the Kaiju wouldn't be returning to finish what they had started. The singular piece of good news amongst the darkness was that Dr. Bach had survived. The Trident that had carried the Doctor and the troops to the island returned to Lemura several hours after the Mother Kaiju had fallen, emerging from the waves and scaring the few soldiers guarding the beachhead against any surviving Kaiju. The Trident had lost its wingman in exchange for the cowardly pilot Knight, and none of the Dogkillers who went to the island returned alive. Conflicting news, to be sure, but Yeltsin was pleased that at least one Trident had survived. A tentative plan had been formed to go see if there were any survivors, but deep down, he was almost certain that there weren't any. In addition, he was reluctant to send the only surviving Trident and its pilots out into the unknown. Not until he had secured the walls of Lemura.

Yeltsin hadn't gotten the chance to see Dr. Bach yet, but doing so was near the top of his list of priorities. Dr. Bach had proven himself an invaluable asset to not only Lemura, but also the continued survival of the human race. His spontaneous creation of a Kaiju "muting" device was being looked at as a defense to be placed in Lemura, amplified by the massive power grid – assuming, he mentally corrected as he slid the report across his desk, the power grid was ever restored.

The light of the rising sun outside his office caught Yeltsin's eye. He shoved aside the piles of work on his desk and moved to the window. Despite the state of the city, for the first time in a long, long while, he realized that he believed mankind stood a decent chance against the monsters from which the oceans had given birth. It was a terrifying feeling, elation.

He smiled. It was not born of fear, or tinged with grimness. It was something he had forgotten, thought lost in the realization of war and extermination. It was a happy smile.

"Long live Lemura."

*****

Deep in the bowels of Marianas Trench, a singular shudder shook the ocean bed around the slumbering beast. Wings, pressed flat against the massive back, twitched ever so slightly. Creatures unseen by humanity's naked eye began to stir amongst the depths. Something caused a far-off underwater volcano to begin erupting, spewing lava and ash into the dark waters. In days, it would begin to form a new island, a new home for a new breed of the dark.

Nothing natural lived at these crushing depths. If Yeltsin had known was lay here, resting, undisturbed for millennia, he may have joined Lemura's Governor in death. Nothing could have prepared him for a creature of such magnitude. It was too large to comprehend, too strange for the mind to accept it. Fortunately, for him, and for all mankind, it remained still as the island formed. Nothing could disturb the creature's sleep yet. Time was not right, reality not quite bent enough for it to arise.

A single eyelid twitched as the beast lay dreaming. Its children began to spawn forth once more, to devour, kill, and to conquer. Slowly from the depths they came to the island of ash and rock to begin anew. It would take a while, but they had time. They settled in beneath the island, these Kaiju.

...and they began to adapt.

Made in the USA
Lexington, KY
14 June 2014